SMALL CLOUD

by Ariane · illustrated by Annie Gusman

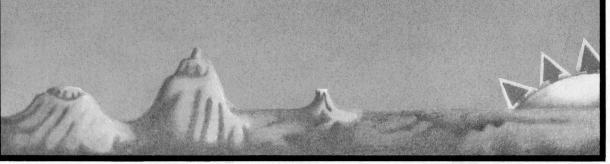

A UNICORN BOOK · E. P. DUTTON · NEW YORK

Library of Congress Cataloging in Publication Data

Ariane.

  Small Cloud.

  "A Unicorn book."

  Summary: As Small Cloud is born to Singing River
and Big Sun, travels across the country, and evolves
into rain, the hydrologic cycle is symbolized.

  [1. Clouds—Fiction.   2. Rain and rainfall—Fiction.
3. Hydrologic cycle—Fiction]   I. Gusman, Annie, ill.
II. Title.

PZ7.A6866Sm   1984   [E]   83-14029
ISBN 0-525-44085-2

Published in the United States by E. P. Dutton, Inc.,
2 Park Avenue, New York, N. Y. 10016

Published simultaneously in Canada by
Fitzhenry & Whiteside Limited, Toronto

Editor: Emilie McLeod   Designer: Riki Levinson

Printed in Hong Kong by South China Printing Co.

First Edition   W   10 9 8 7 6 5 4 3 2 1

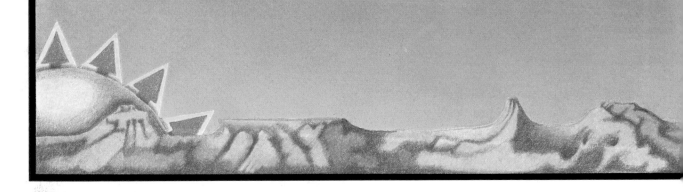

for Lilia and Serena
and all Children of the Earth
A.

for Emilie McLeod
A.G.

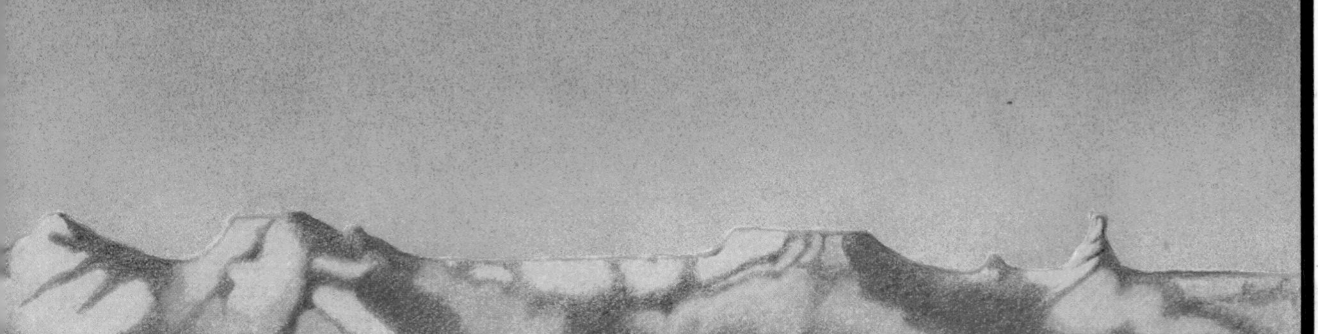

In the beginning, there was Small Cloud's mother, Singing River, and her father, Big Sun.

One day Singing River called to Big Sun.
Big Sun smiled and warmed the heart of Singing River.
Singing River danced in the warmth, and a mist rose slowly into the air.

One drop at a time, Small Cloud was born.

When she was grown, she called to Singing River,
"I want to go over the mountain."
"Yes," Singing River sighed. "If Whistling Wind
will help you, and if your father, Big Sun, will
watch over you, I will wait for you."

"What lies beyond the mountain?" Small Cloud asked.
"The world," Big Sun told her.
"What is the world?" Small Cloud asked.
"Come," said Whistling Wind, "I will show you."

And he lifted Small Cloud up over the mountain
and into a valley.
"Here corn grows," Whistling Wind told her.
"Someday you may help it."
Small Cloud's shadow swooped down into
the valley and then over another mountain
to a desert.
Whistling Wind blew her across the hot earth.
"Go quickly," Big Sun urged her. "Here there is
no one to help."

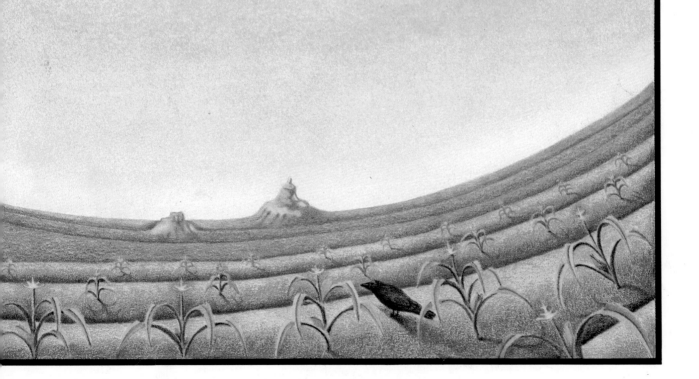

Small Cloud sped over the desert and came to a
lake where other small clouds played.
"They are just like me!" Small Cloud said.
"Go to them," said Whistling Wind. "They will
play with you."

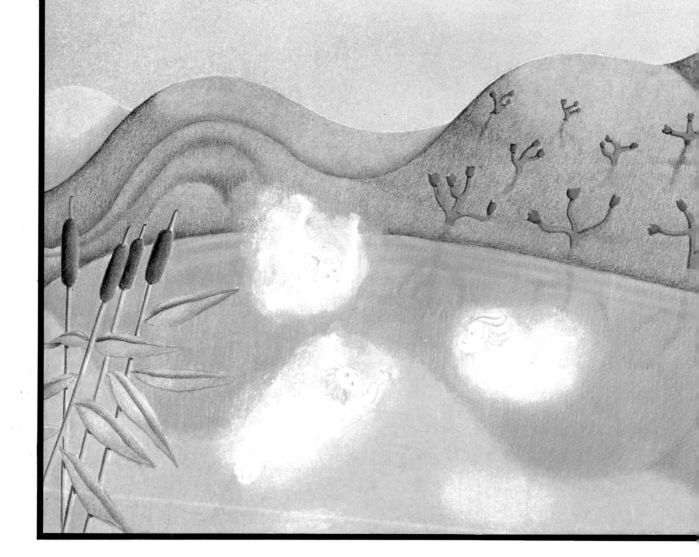

Small Cloud and her friends chased each other above the lake.
Then, with a great gust, Whistling Wind lifted them high over the mountains and into another valley. "The corn is dry and the creatures are sad," said Whistling Wind. "The earth needs rain."

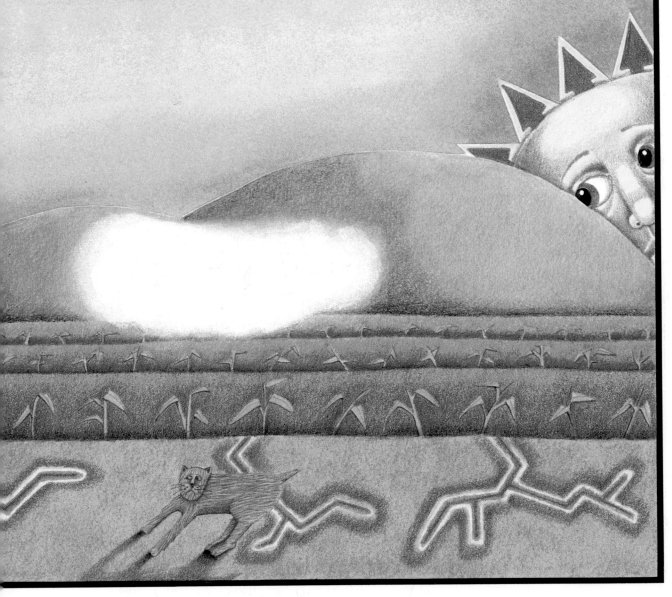

Small Cloud and her friends moved across
the sky and into each other. Together,
they became one great cloud, and rain
began to fall.
Drop by drop, Small Cloud and her friends
gave themselves to the earth.

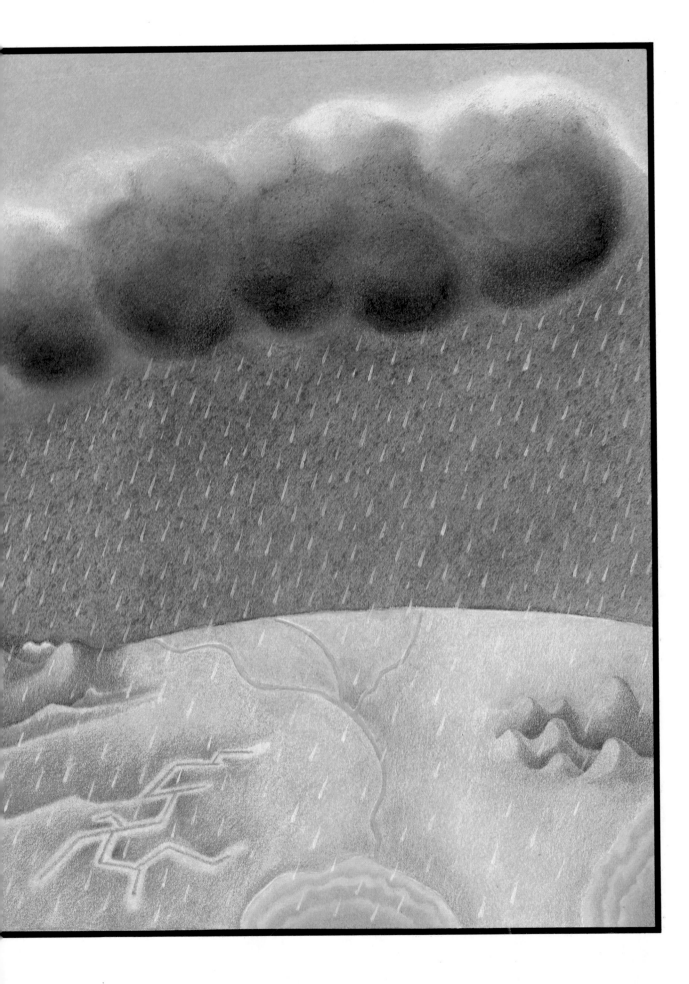

When the earth was full and the corn <u>satisfied</u>, Small
Cloud gave her last raindrop to a river.
As Small Cloud disappeared, she heard Singing
River call out, "Big Sun! Small Cloud has come
home."
Big Sun smiled and warmed the heart of Singing
River.

Singing River danced in the warmth, and a mist
rose slowly into the air.
One drop at a time, Small Cloud was born again.